MW00906580

Little Giant—Children's Bible Classics
Copyright © 1992 by Educational Publishing Concepts, Inc.
All rights reserved. No portion of this book may be reproduced in any form, except for brief quotations in reviews, without written permission from the publisher.

Illustrations © 1979-1983 Bible Discovery Aids;
owners: Sweet Publishing, Fort Worth, TX, and
Gospel Light, Regal Books, Ventura, CA.

(ISBN 0-529-07194-0)
Printed in Singapore

CONTENTS

JESUS IS BORN

JESUS' EARLY MINISTRY

JESUS TEACHES AND HEALS

Mary's Visitor Luke 1:26-56; Matthew 1:18-25

God had sent an angel to a man named Zechariah to tell him that he and his wife Elizabeth would have a baby. At this time, God often spoke to His people in this way.

A month later God's angel visited a girl in Nazareth named Mary. This girl was a relative of Zechariah and Elizabeth. The angel said, "Peace to you Mary. God is very happy with you and He has decided to bless you."

6

"Very soon you are going to have a baby boy. You are to name Him Jesus. He will be very great and will be called the Son of God. He will be a King and His kingdom will last forever."

Mary was confused. "How can this happen? I'm not even
married yet!" Mary was engaged to be married to a man
named Joseph. The angel answered, "God's Spirit will
rest upon you, so the baby will be called God's Son."

"I am God's servant and I will do whatever He wants,"
Mary replied. Then the angel disappeared.

9

A few days later Mary went to visit her relative Elizabeth. When Mary called out a greeting, the baby inside Elizabeth jumped. The Holy Spirit filled Elizabeth with joy.

10

Elizabeth hugged Mary and cried, "You are truly blessed by God and favored over all other women. Your baby shall have God's greatest praise!"

Mary said, "My heart rejoices in God. Because He noticed me and gave me this honor, people will always call me blessed of God." Mary stayed with Elizabeth three months before returning home.

12

Meanwhile Mary's fiance Joseph heard that she was going to have a baby. This news made him unhappy and he decided to quietly break his engagement to Mary.

But one night Joseph had a dream. In it an angel was standing and talking to him. "Joseph, don't be afraid to take Mary as your wife. The baby that she is going to have is from the Holy Spirit."

14

"Mary's baby will be a boy and you shall name Him Jesus because He will save His people from their sins." When Joseph woke up from this dream he did as the angel said and brought Mary home to be his wife.

Everything happened this way so that what God had told the prophet Isaiah to write would come true: "A virgin will have a baby and they will call Him Immanuel which means God with us."

Jesus Is Born Luke 2:1-38

Several months had passed since the angel had said Mary would have a baby. Now Mary and Joseph were married and lived in Nazareth. The Roman emperor, Augustus wanted to count how many people lived in their land.

Everyone had to go to the town that their ancestors were from for this census. So Joseph and Mary headed for Bethlehem. This town in Judea was where King David, Joseph's ancestor had lived.

18

Soon after they got to Bethlehem, Mary had her baby.
Joseph hadn't been able to get them a room because all
the inns were full, so they were staying in a stable.
When the baby was born, Mary laid Him in a manger.

That same night some shepherds were watching their flocks outside of town. Suddenly an angel appeared to them. The sky was filled with the glory of the Lord and the shepherds were very afraid!

The angel said, "Don't be afraid! I am bringing you good news that today in the city of David, your Savior has been born. He is the Messiah, the Lord, and you will find Him lying in a manger."

When the angel had disappeared the shepherds hurried into Bethlehem. They found Joseph and Mary and the tiny baby lying in a manger.

The shepherds told them what the angel had said about
the baby. Everyone was amazed by these words. But
Mary heard these things and kept them in her heart.
She often thought about what the angel had said.

When the baby was eight days old He was circumcised, as was the custom. At this ceremony He was named Jesus, just as the angel had told Mary and Joseph He should be.

Forty days later Joseph and Mary went to the temple in
Jerusalem to make a sacrifice. The law's requirement
was for either two doves or two pigeons. In the temple,
they met an old man named Simeon.

Simeon was a good man who prayed often for the
Messiah to come and save Israel. The Holy Spirit had
told him that he would not die until he had seen God's
chosen King.

26

Simeon took little Jesus in his arms and said, "Lord God You have kept Your promise. Now I can die in peace because I have seen Your Savior."

He turned to Mary and said, "This Child will be a great joy to many people, but many others will reject Him and speak against Him. Because of this your own heart will be broken."

The Wise Men Come Matthew 2

About the time that Jesus was born some wise men in a country to the east saw a mysterious star. They began to follow the star because they thought it would lead them to a king.

They arrived in Jerusalem and began asking questions. "Where is the child who will be king of the Jews? We saw His star and have come to worship Him."

Herod, the king of Judea was upset about these questions. He didn't want any new king taking his kingdom. He called in his chief priests and teachers, "Do the prophets say where this king will be born?" he asked.

"Yes," they answered. He will be born in Bethlehem. We
know this because the prophet Micah wrote, 'Out of
you, O Bethlehem, will come a shepherd for my people
Israel.' "

32

Herod met with the wise men. He wanted to know exactly when they had seen the star. Then he said, "When you find this child King, come back and tell me where He is so that I may go and worship Him, too."

As the wise men left Jerusalem, the star appeared before them again. They were thrilled and they followed the star until it led them to where Jesus was.

When the wise men went into the house where Mary and Joseph lived, they saw Jesus. They bowed down and worshiped Him and gave Him the gifts they had brought--gold, frankincense, and myrrh.

When the wise men left Bethlehem, they did not return
to King Herod. They had been warned in a dream to go a
different way. King Herod did not really want to worship
Jesus, instead he wanted to kill Him.

36

An angel also warned Joseph in a dream. The angel said, "Joseph take Mary and the Child and go to Egypt. King Herod is going to try to kill Jesus, so stay there until I tell you that it is safe to return."

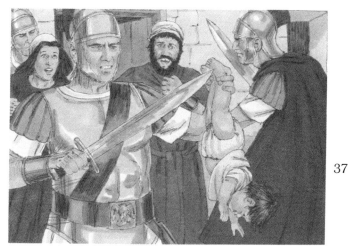

Herod soon realized that the wise men were not coming back. He was very angry. He knew that Jesus was not yet two years old, so he ordered his soldiers to kill all the boys in Bethlehem who were two years and under.

38

A while later, King Herod died. Then the angel came to Joseph again and said, "You can take Jesus back to the land of Israel now. It is safe for Him to be there".

Joseph got up and took Mary and Jesus back to Israel.
He was afraid to go to Judea because Herod's son was
the new ruler, so they went to the town of Nazareth
which was in Galilee.

Jesus as a Boy Luke 2:40-52

Joseph had taken Mary and Jesus to Egypt because an angel had warned him that King Herod wanted to harm Jesus. After the death of King Herod, the little family returned to Israel and settled in Nazareth in Galilee.

So Jesus lived in the small town of Nazareth with His family. He enjoyed doing the same things other children did. He grew to be a strong boy and wiser than other children His age. God blessed Him very much.

42

When Jesus was twelve years old, Mary and Joseph took Him with them on their annual trip to Jerusalem. Every year they went there to celebrate the Passover Festival.

When the Passover celebration ended Mary and Joseph started home. They were traveling with many friends and relatives from Nazareth. Jesus wasn't with them, but they thought He was walking with His friends.

44

After traveling for about a day, Mary and Joseph realized they hadn't seen Jesus at all. They asked around
but no one had seen Him. So Mary and Joseph headed
back to Jerusalem.

They searched around the city for three days. Finally they found Jesus in the Temple! He had stayed behind to talk with the teachers of the Law.

Jesus was sitting in the middle of all the teachers. He was asking them questions and even answering questions. Everyone was amazed at how much He understood.

Mary and Joseph didn't know what to think. They were
very surprised to find Jesus there.

48

"Son," Mary said, "Why did You do this to us? Your father and I have been looking everywhere for You. We were very worried!"

Jesus answered, "Why did you need to look for Me? Didn't you know that I would be here in My Father's house?" But Mary and Joseph didn't really understand what Jesus meant.

50

Jesus returned to Nazareth with Mary and Joseph. He was always obedient to them. Mary always remembered these things.

Jesus continued to grow tall and wise. He was loved by God and man.

Jesus Is Tempted Matthew 3:13-4:11

John the Baptist traveled around telling people to turn away from their sins and be baptized, then God would forgive them. One time he was preaching near the Jordan River. Many people listened and were baptized.

Jesus was one of the people who came to the Jordan
River to be baptized by John. When he saw Jesus, John
was surprised. "This isn't right," John said, "I should be
baptized by You!"

54

Jesus replied, "Please baptize Me, this is the right thing to do." So John agreed to baptize Jesus.

As Jesus came up out of the water He saw the Spirit of God in the form of a dove come down on Him. Then a voice from heaven said, "This is My beloved Son and I am very pleased with Him!"

56

After this the Holy Spirit took Jesus out into the desert. For forty days and forty nights Jesus ate nothing and became very hungry. Suddenly the devil came to see if he could make Jesus sin.

The devil knew that Jesus was very hungry, so he said, "Go ahead turn these stones into bread. That would prove that You are the Son of God."

58

Jesus answered, "No! The Scriptures tell us that man does not live by bread alone but by the words that God speaks."

59

Next the devil took Jesus to the top of the Temple in Jerusalem. "Throw Yourself down from here," he said. "The Scriptures say that God will send His angels to keep You from harm."

60

Jesus responded, "The Scriptures also say not to put the Lord your God to a test!"

Then the devil took Jesus to the top of a very high mountain. He showed Him all the nations of the world. "I will give this all to You, if You will kneel down and worship me," the devil said.

62

Jesus said, "Get out of here, Satan. The Scriptures say,
'Worship only the Lord God and serve only Him.' "

63

Finally the devil left and angels came and cared for Jesus.

Jesus Chooses Disciples John 1:35-51

When Jesus had come to John and asked to be baptized,
John didn't want to do it. But Jesus told him that this
was what God wanted, so John baptized Him.

The next day John was talking with two of his followers when he saw Jesus coming. "Look," he said. "There goes the Lamb of God."

66

When they heard this the two men followed after Jesus.
When Jesus turned around and saw them He asked,
"What do you want?" "Teacher, where are You staying?"
they asked.

"Come and see," Jesus said. So they went home with
Jesus. This was at about 4 o'clock in the afternoon.
They spent the rest of the evening talking with Jesus.

One of these men was Andrew, the brother of Simon Peter. As soon as Andrew left Jesus he went to find Simon. "Come with me," he said. "We have found the Messiah (which means the Christ)."

Andrew took Simon to where Jesus was. Jesus looked at Simon for a few minutes. Then Jesus said, "You are Simon, John's son, but now you shall be called Peter which means 'the rock.' "

The next day Jesus decided to go to Galilee. He found a man named Philip and told him, "Come with Me." Philip was from the same town as Andrew and Peter, the town of Bethsaida.

Philip hurried off to find Nathanael. "We have found the Messiah," he told him. "The very one that Moses and the prophets wrote about. He is Jesus of Nazareth."

"Nazareth!" shouted Nathanael. "Can anything good come from there?" "Just come and see for yourself," Philip answered.

Jesus saw Nathanael coming with Philip and said,
"Here comes an honest man, a true Israelite."

74

"How can You say that?" Nathanael asked. "You don't even know me." Jesus answered, "I saw you sitting under the fig tree before Philip ever found you."

Nathanael was amazed. "Sir, You are truly the Son of God, the King of Israel!" Jesus answered, "Do you believe just because I said I saw you under the fig tree? You will see more wonderful things than this!"

The Miracle at Cana John 2:1-12

Jesus had now chosen four men to be His disciples.
There were two brothers, Andrew and Simon Peter,
and two other men, Philip and Nathanael.

A short time after they began traveling with Jesus they were all invited to a wedding celebration in a small village called Cana. Jesus' mother was also at the wedding.

78

During the celebration the host ran out of wine for the guests. This could be very embarrassing for him and Jesus' mother wanted to help. She went to Jesus and told Him about the problem.

Jesus said, "I can't help you with this problem. My time to do miracles has not come yet." But Jesus' mother turned to the servants and said, "Do whatever He tells you to do."

80

Jesus noticed six stone water jars standing nearby.
These big pots were used by the Jews for ceremonial
washing. Each jar would hold about twenty or thirty
gallons of water.

"Fill these jars with water," Jesus instructed the servants. So the men completely filled each jar.

When they were finished He said, "Now take some out and give it to the host of this celebration."

The man in charge of the wedding feast tasted the water, which had now been turned into wine. He didn't know where this wine had come from, but of course the servants knew.

He called the bridegroom aside and said, "This wine is terrific! Most people serve the best wine first."

"Then when all the guests have had alot to drink they bring out the cheaper wine. No one cares then anyway. But, you have saved the best wine for now!"

86

This miracle at Cana was Jesus' first public miracle that showed who He really was. His glory was revealed and His disciples truly believed He was the Messiah.

When the wedding was over, Jesus went down to Capernaum for a few days with His mother and His brothers and His disciples.

The Woman at the Well John 4:3-42

Jesus and His disciples had spent a few days in
Capernaum after attending a wedding in Cana. Then
they went to Jerusalem for the Passover celebration.
When this was over they started home to Galilee.

During their journey they came to a town in Samaria
called Sychar. Jesus was tired so He sat down to rest
by a well known as Jacob's Well. His disciples went into
town to buy some food.

90

Soon a Samaritan woman came to the well to draw some water. "Will you give Me a drink?" Jesus asked. The woman was surprised because Jews hated Samaritans and didn't usually speak to them. She said this to Jesus.

Jesus said, "If you knew what a wonderful gift God has for you, and who I am you would have asked Me for 'living water.' " "But You don't have a rope or a bucket. How can You get water from this deep well?" she asked.

92

"I'm not talking about this water," Jesus said. "Everyone who drinks this water will get thirsty again. But whoever drinks the water I give will never be thirsty again."

"Sir," she said. "Give me some of that water, then I won't have to make the long walk to this well every day." Jesus said, "Go get your husband and bring him to Me."

94

"I don't have a husband," the woman said. Jesus replied, "That is the truth. But you have had five husbands, and you are not married to the man you are living with now."

The woman didn't want to talk about this so she asked a new question. "Why is it that you Jews say we have to worship God in Jerusalem, but my ancestors say the right place to worship is here on this mountain?"

96

Jesus replied, "The time is coming when it will not matter where you worship, but how you worship. True worshipers will worship God in spirit and in truth. That is the kind of worship God wants from us."

The woman said, "At least I know that one day the Messiah will come and He will explain everything to us." Then Jesus quietly said, "I am He."

The woman ran back to town, even forgetting her water jar. She called to everyone, "Come and see. There is a Man who told me everything I ever did. Can He be the Messiah?" Many people came to see Jesus.

Some Samaritans believed in Jesus just because of what the woman had said. Jesus stayed and talked with them for two days. After that many more believed because they had heard His words themselves.

Jesus Chooses More Disciples Mark 2:13-17; 3:13-19

Jesus had already called six men to follow Him as disciples. They were Simon Peter, Andrew, James, John, Philip, and Nathanael. These six men traveled everywhere with Jesus.

One day Jesus had been speaking to a crowd of people near the Sea of Galilee. As He was leaving He noticed a booth where the Jews paid taxes to the Romans. One of the tax collectors was a Jew.

Jesus went up to this man and said, "Follow Me." The man immediately got up and went with Jesus. This tax collector was named Levi, though some called him Matthew.

That night Levi invited many of his friends to come for dinner and to meet Jesus and His disciples. Many of his friends were tax collectors like him and they had a reputation for being sinners.

104

Some of the Jewish religious leaders, called Pharisees, saw Jesus sitting with this crowd of men. The Pharisees didn't like these men because they didn't carefully follow Jewish laws.

So the angry Pharisees went to Jesus' disciples and asked, "Why is your Master eating with tax collectors and sinners?"

106

Jesus heard their question and He answered it Himself, "People who are well do not need a doctor, but sick people do. I haven't come to talk to people who are already doing right, but to those who are sinning."

One day, some time later, Jesus went up into the mountains. He spent the night praying. The next day He invited some of His followers to join Him on the mountain.

108

Jesus chose twelve of these followers to be His apostles or special messengers. These twelve included: Simon, now called Peter, his brother Andrew, James and his brother John (called Sons of Thunder).

Philip and Bartholomew (this may be another name for
Nathanael), Matthew (this was Levi the tax collector),
Thomas, James the son of Alphaeus,

Thaddaeus (also called Judas, the son of James), and
Simon the Zealot. There was one more apostle; Judas
Iscariot, the man who would later betray Jesus.

These twelve men were Jesus' companions. They went out and preached and He gave them the power to heal the sick and to cast out demons. They were trained to carry on Jesus' work.

Guidelines for Living Matthew 5-7

Jesus became more and more famous and people came from everywhere to see Him and hear Him speak. One day He went up on a mountainside to talk with His disciples. Crowds of people gathered to listen also.

"Blessed are the poor in spirit, for theirs is the kingdom of heaven. Blessed are the pure in heart, for they shall see God. Blessed are the peacemakers, for they will be called children of God."

114

"I have not come to do away with the Law or the Prophets; I have come to fulfill them. He who breaks even one commandment will be called the least in heaven, but He who keeps the commandments will be called the greatest in heaven."

"You have heard that Moses law taught, 'Do not murder, anyone who murders will be judged.' But I am
telling you that anyone who is even angry with his
brother will be judged."

116

"You have heard it said, 'An eye for an eye and a tooth for a tooth.' But I am telling you if an evil person hits you, don't resist him, turn your other cheek for him to hit also."

"You have heard the saying, 'Love your neighbor and hate your enemy.' But I say, even sinners do that, you should love your enemies and pray for those who hurt you, then you will be acting like sons of God."

118

"When you give to the needy, don't do what the hypocrites do, shouting about it and blowing trumpets so everyone will notice. The truth is the praise they get from men is the only reward they will receive."

"Do not store treasures for yourself here on earth, where moths and rust will destroy them or thieves may steal them. But store up treasures for yourself in heaven. Where your treasure is, there your heart will be also."

120

"Ask and it shall be given to you; seek and you will find; knock and the door will be opened to you. Anyone who asks, receives; anyone who seeks, finds; and to the one who knocks, the door will be opened."

"In everything, do to others what you would like them
to do for you. This is the heart of the teaching of the
Law of Moses and the Prophets."

122

"Watch out for fake teachers, not everyone who says to me 'Lord, Lord' will enter the kingdom of heaven, but only the ones who do the will of My Father who is in heaven."

When Jesus had finished teaching, the crowds were amazed. He didn't teach like their Jewish leaders, but He spoke as one who had great authority.

Jesus Shows God's Power *Mark 4:35-41*

One day Jesus said to His disciples, "Let's go to the other side of the sea."

So they left the crowds who were following Jesus and got into a boat. They began sailing across the sea along with some other boats.

As they were sailing across the Sea of Galilee, a big storm suddenly came up. The waves began to pound against the boat and water began pouring into it.

127

The disciples were very afraid, but Jesus was in the
back of the boat sound asleep! They ran to Him and
woke Him up. "Master, don't You care that we may all
die? Save us!" they cried.

128

Jesus stood up and called out to the wind and the sea, "Quiet, be still!"

As soon as He said this, the storm stopped and the sea became very quiet. Then Jesus turned to His disciples, "Why were you afraid? Don't you have any confidence in Me?"

130

The disciples were filled with awe. They turned to each other asking, "Who is this Man that even the wind and the sea obey Him?"

Another time a man who was possessed by a demon
was brought to Jesus. The man could not see or speak.
Jesus cast the demon out and healed the man.

132

The crowd of people were amazed and they wondered where Jesus got His power. The Pharisees quickly answered, "He is able to cast out demons because He has the power of Beelzebub, the prince of demons."

Jesus knew what they were thinking so He said, "Any kingdom that is divided against itself will be ruined. Therefore if Satan is giving Me the power to cast out demons, how can his kingdom survive?"

134

"And if My power is from Beelzebub, what about your own followers? Who gives them the power to cast out demons?"

135

"But if it is by God's power that I am driving out
demons, then that shows that the kingdom of God has
arrived. It shows that One who is stronger than Satan
is here and is overcoming the prince of darkness."

"She Is Just Asleep" *Mark 5:21-43*

Jesus was speaking to a large crowd of people when one of the rulers of the synagogue, a man named Jairus, came to Him.

The man fell at Jesus' feet and begged, "Please come home with me. My daughter is dying and I know that You can put Your hands on her and she will live." So Jesus went with the man.

The huge crowd followed Jesus and pushed in close around Him. In the crowd was a woman who had been ill for twelve years. She had a bleeding problem and had spent nearly all her money on doctors.

She came up close to Jesus in the crowd, thinking that if she could just touch His clothes, she would be healed. When she managed to touch His robe, she could feel inside that her body had truly been healed!

140

But Jesus was also aware that something had happened. He quickly turned around and said, "Who touched My clothes?" "Look at all these people, how can You ask that?" His disciples responded.

Jesus kept looking at all the people in the crowd until the woman finally came forward. She fearfully told Jesus about herself. When He had heard her story He said, "Your faith has made you well. Go in peace."

142

While this was all going on, some men from the household of Jairus arrived. They said, "Your daughter is dead, so you do not need to bother the Teacher anymore."

Jesus ignored their words and turned to Jairus. He
gently said, "Don't be afraid, just believe." Then
Jesus took Peter, James, and John with Him to
Jairus' house.

144

When they arrived, people there were crying and wailing loudly. Jesus said, "Why are you crying and wailing? The child is not dead, but just asleep." They all laughed at Him.

145

Jesus told everyone to leave the house except Peter, James, and John and the girl's parents. Then He went into the room where the girl was laying.

He took the child's small hand in His and said, "Little girl, get up!" Immediately the child stood up and began walking around. She was about twelve years old.

147

The girl's parents were astonished! Jesus told them not to tell anyone what had happened. Then He said, "Give her something to eat."

The Miracle Lunch *Mark 6:30-44*

Jesus taught His disciples, then sent them out to preach to the people. When they returned Jesus said, "Come away with Me. Let's go away for a while, we need a rest."

So they got on a boat and began to sail for the other side of the Sea of Galilee. However, some of the people saw them leave.

150

These people began to run along the shore of the sea until they got to the place where Jesus was going. So, when the boat landed there was a large crowd of people there to meet them.

Jesus felt sorry for the people, He knew that they
needed His help. So He began to teach them and even
healed some of the sick ones.

152

Soon evening came and the disciples said, "Tell the people to go to the nearby villages and buy food. It is starting to get late and there is nothing here to eat."

153

But Jesus said, "No, YOU feed them." The disciples
were shocked at this order.

154

They said, "It would take a fortune to buy food for all these people. Do You want us to spend all our money on food?"

"Go see how much food we have," Jesus ordered. The disciples searched through the crowd and came back with a small boy. He had brought a lunch of five loaves of bread and two fish.

156

Then Jesus told the big crowd of people to sit down on the grass. He asked them to sit in groups of fifty or a hundred people. There were five thousand men, and that wasn't counting the women and children!

Jesus took the bread and fish that the little boy had
given. He lifted it up to heaven and gave thanks to
God for it.

Then Jesus broke the bread and fish into pieces. He gave it to the disciples and they began passing it out to the people. There was plenty of food and everyone ate all they wanted.

When everyone was finished, the disciples gathered up
the leftovers. There were twelve full baskets of bread
and fish left over!

Jesus Walks on the Water *Matthew 14:22-33*

After Jesus had fed the crowd of five thousand people,
He told His disciples to get into the boat and go to the
other side of the Sea of Galilee.

Jesus stayed behind to encourage the crowd to go home. When the people had left He went up into the hills by Himself to pray.

162

When evening came, He was still praying, alone on a hill. The disciples' boat was now out in the middle of the Sea of Galilee.

A strong wind had come up out on the sea and Jesus could see that the disciples were having a hard time. They were trying to row the boat, but the wind was blowing them in the wrong direction.

Around 3 or 4 o'clock in the morning the disciples looked up and saw a man coming to them. He was walking on top of the water!

When they saw the man walking on top of the water, the disciples were very afraid. They thought it was a ghost!

166

Jesus reassured them immediately, "Don't be afraid.
Have courage, it is I!"

Peter said, "Lord, if it is really You, tell me to come to You on the water." "Alright," Jesus said, "Come!"

168

Then Peter went over the side of the boat and began walking on the water toward Jesus!

169

But when Peter looked around and saw the wind, he was afraid and he started to sink. He cried, "Lord, save me!"

Instantly Jesus reached out and caught Peter's hand.
"O you of little faith, why did you doubt?" He asked.

When Jesus and Peter got into the boat the wind stopped blowing and the sea was calm. The amazed disciples whispered, "You really are the Son of God." And they all worshiped Him.

Jesus Is Changed *Matthew 16:13-21; 17:1-13*

Once when they were at a place called Caesarea Phillipi, Jesus asked His disciples, "Who do you think I am?" Peter answered, "You are the Christ, the Son of God." Then Jesus told them all that would happen to Him.

About a week after this, Jesus took Peter, James, and John with Him. They went up on a tall mountain all alone.

174

Jesus began praying and right in front of them, He was transfigured, or changed in His appearance. His clothes became as white as light and His face was shining like the sun.

Suddenly Elijah and Moses appeared and began talking to Jesus. They were discussing the things that would happen to Him later in Jerusalem.

176

Peter was awestruck. He said, "Lord let me build three booths. One for You and one for Moses and one for Elijah."

As Peter was speaking, they were all covered by a
bright cloud. A voice spoke from the cloud. It said,
"This is My Son. I love Him and am pleased with
Him. Listen to Him."

178

The disciples were terrified and fell down on the ground. But Jesus came and touched them and said, "Get up, don't be afraid." When they looked up He was alone.

As they were going down the mountain, Jesus told them, "Don't tell anyone what you have seen here until the Son of man is raised from the dead."

180

The disciples were confused and they asked, "Then why do the Jewish teachers say that Elijah must come first before the Messiah comes?"

181

"Elijah does come and he will restore all things,"
Jesus answered.

182

"But he has come already and no one recognized him. He was mistreated by many people."

"In much the same way, the Son of man will suffer at their hands." The disciples understood that He was talking about John the Baptist.

Jesus Gives Sight *John 9*

One day Jesus saw a man who had been blind all his life. His disciples asked Him, "Master, was this man born blind because of his own sins or those of his parents?"

Jesus' answer surprised them, "It was not because of either of their sins. This man was born blind so that the power of God might be demonstrated in his life."

Jesus spat on the ground and made mud. He rubbed some of the mud on the man's eyes. Next He told the man, "Go and wash in the pool of Siloam."

The man did what Jesus said and when he came back, he could see! Everyone who knew him was amazed. "Is this the blind man who used to sit and beg?" they asked. "Yes, I am the same one," the man replied.

188

He told them what Jesus had done. Then they took him to the Pharisees and he told his story again. This all happened on the Sabbath day, so the Pharisees said, "Jesus is not from God or He would keep the Sabbath."

But other people asked, "How could a sinner do such miracles?" Then they went back to the man who had been blind. "What do you say about Him?" they asked. "I think He must be a prophet," the man answered.

190

The Jewish leaders wouldn't believe the man had been born blind, so they sent for his parents. They began to question them, "Is this your son? Was he born blind? How come he can see now?"

The parents replied, "Yes, he is our son and he was born blind. We don't know why he can see now. Ask him, he can give his own answers." The Pharisees turned to the man and said, "This Jesus is a sinner."

192

The man answered, "I don't know about that, I just
know that I was blind, but now I can see." So they
asked him to repeat his story again. "Why?" he asked,
"Do you want to be His disciples too?"

This made the Pharisees very angry. They shouted,
"You are His disciple, but we are disciples of Moses.
We know God spoke to Moses, but we don't know
about this Jesus." And they threw the man out
of the synagogue.

194

Jesus heard what had happened and went to the man. He found him and asked, "Do you believe in the Messiah?" The man answered, "Who is He? I want to believe."

195

Jesus said, "You have seen Him. In fact He is speaking to you right now." The man fell to his knees and said, "I believe." Then he worshiped Jesus.

The Good Neighbor *Luke 10:25-37*

One day a teacher of the Jewish law came to Jesus. He wanted to ask Him a question to test Him.

"Teacher," he said. "What do I have to do to live forever in heaven?" Jesus answered him with a question, "What does the law say? How do you understand it?"

198

The teacher answered, "It says love the Lord your God with all your heart, and with all your soul, and with all your strength, and all your mind. And you should love your neighbor as yourself."

"That's right," Jesus said, "Do this and you will live."
But the teacher wanted to impress Jesus, so he asked,
"Well, who is my neighbor?"

200

Jesus answered him by telling a story. "There was a Jewish man traveling down from Jerusalem to Jericho."

"Suddenly some robbers attacked him. They beat him up and took his clothes. He was nearly dead when they finally left."

202

"Soon a Jewish priest came down the road. He saw the man lying there, but he didn't stop to help. He crossed to the other side of the road and kept right on going."

"A short time later a Jewish temple worker came down the road. He saw the poor man who had been robbed and beaten. But instead of helping him, he crossed the road and kept walking."

"Finally a Samaritan man came along. He saw the man lying there, and even though the Jews and Samaritans don't get along, he felt sorry for him. He stopped and put medicine on the man's wounds and bandaged them."

"He put the man on his donkey and took him to the nearest inn. He stayed with the man all night, caring for him."

206

"The next morning the Samaritan had to leave, but he gave money to the innkeeper with these instructions, 'Take care of this man. If you spend more than this, I will pay you back when I return.' "

Now Jesus asked the man, "Which of these three men was a neighbor to the man who was robbed?" "It was the one who helped him," the man answered. "You go and do the same," Jesus said.

The Parable of the Lost Son *Luke 15:11-32*

The Pharisees were still criticizing Jesus for nearly everything He did. They said, "He goes around with sinners and tax collectors. He even eats with them." So Jesus told them a kind of story called a parable.

209

"There was once a man who had two sons. The younger son came to his father one day and said, 'I want my share of inheritance now.' So the father divided all he owned and gave half to the younger son."

"Soon after that the younger son decided he wanted to get away from home. So he took all his money and headed for another country far way. But, when he got there he wasted all his money on parties and wild living."

"Then a great famine came over that land and there was very little food for anyone. Since the younger son had no money, he needed a job. He found one feeding pigs. But often he was so hungry that he wanted the pigs' food."

212

"Finally the younger son realized that back at home even his father's workers had food to eat. 'I will go back to father and admit my mistake. Then maybe he will let me be one of his workers.'"

213

"So he returned home. His father saw him coming when he was still some way from home and he was filled with pity for his son. He ran to the younger son and hugged and kissed him."

214

" 'Father,' the son said, 'I have sinned against God and you. I am no longer worthy of being called your son.' "

"But the father called to his servants, 'Bring a robe, a ring, and shoes for my son. Kill the best calf we have to make a feast! My son was dead, but now he is alive, he was lost, but now he is found!' "

216

"The older son was in the fields working. When he heard all the celebrating he asked someone what was going on and they told him that his brother was home. This made him angry and he wouldn't join the party."

"His father came out and begged him. But the older son said, 'Father, I have worked hard for you all these years and I have always obeyed you. But you never gave me a party.' "

218

" 'Now my brother comes home after wasting your
money on wild living and you kill our best calf and
throw a great celebration for him.' "

"The father replied, 'Son, you are always here and you may have anything that I own. But your brother was dead, and now he is alive again. It is right that we celebrate this.' "

The Story of Lazarus John 11:1-54

The small village of Bethany was about two miles from Jerusalem. Some good friends of Jesus lived in Bethany. They were two sisters, Mary and Martha, and their brother Lazarus.

One day the sisters sent a very important message to Jesus. Lazarus was very sick and the sisters knew that Jesus could make him well. They hoped that Jesus would come to Bethany as soon as possible.

But Jesus waited two days before telling the disciples that He was going to Bethany. They were not happy about this trip because some men had tried to kill Jesus the last time He had gone there. "We must go," Jesus said, "Lazarus needs Me."

When Jesus arrived in Bethany, Martha ran to meet Him. She said, "Lazarus is dead. I know that he would still be alive if You had been here, but I also know that God will do anything You ask Him to, even now."

224

Jesus said, "I am the One who gives life, anyone who believes in Me will live again, even if he dies. Do you believe this, Martha?" "Yes," she answered, "You are the Son of God."

Martha sent for Mary to come and see Jesus. All the friends who were comforting Mary came also. Everyone was crying. Mary said, "Jesus, if You had been here my brother would not have died." Jesus was very sad and He cried, too.

226

They took Jesus to the cave where Lazarus was buried.
"Roll away the stone that covers the door!" Jesus said.
"Wait!" Martha said, "He has been dead four days, by
now there will be a bad smell."

Jesus answered, "Remember I told you that if you believed you would see the wonderful greatness of God?" So they rolled the big stone away.

228

Then Jesus looked up to heaven and prayed, "Thank You Father, for hearing Me. I know that You always hear Me, but I want all these people standing here to know that too, so that they may believe that You have sent Me."

After He had prayed, Jesus looked at the cave. In a loud voice He called, "Lazarus, come out!"

230

Suddenly, Lazarus walked out of the cave. He was still covered with strips of cloth, but he was alive! "Take off the grave clothes and let him go," Jesus commanded.

Many who saw this miracle believed in Jesus that day.
But some people reported it to the Pharisees. They
hated Jesus, so they called a meeting of the Jewish
Council and talked about ways to kill Him.

The Rich Young Man *Mark 10:17-31*

Jesus was in Judea, east of the Jordan River. As always crowds of people came to Him and He spoke with them and taught them.

Then, as Jesus was leaving for Jerusalem one day a man came up to Him. The man kneeled down before Jesus and asked, "Good Teacher, what must I do to be saved and go to heaven?"

234

Jesus said, "Why do you call Me good? No one is good except God. But, to answer your question, you know the commandments: do not murder, do not lie, do not steal, honor your father and mother. . . ."

The man replied, "Teacher, I have kept all these laws since I was a small child." Jesus looked at the man and felt a real love for him.

"There is one thing you lack," Jesus said. "Go and sell everything you own and give the money to the poor, then your treasure will be in heaven. Then come and follow Me."

When the young man heard this he became sad because he was very rich. He got up and slowly walked away.

238

Jesus looked around at His disciples and said, "It is very hard for a rich man to get into the kingdom of heaven."

The disciples were shocked even more when Jesus added, "It would be easier for a camel to go through the eye of a needle than for a rich man to enter God's kingdom."

One of the disciples asked, "If the rich can't be saved, who can?" Jesus responded, "With men it is completely impossible, but with God all things are possible."

Peter said, "We have all left everything we had and followed You."

242

Jesus answered, "Anyone who leaves his home or brothers and sisters and mother and father or fields for Me and to tell the Good News will receive much more in this age."

"He will have a hundred times more houses, brothers, sisters, mothers, fathers, and fields, and with them will come persecutions. But in the age to come, he will have eternal life!"

Two Men Are Saved Mark 10:46-52

One time Jesus was leaving Jericho and a great crowd of people was following Him. Along the side of the road there was a blind man named Bartimaeus, begging for money.

Bartimaeus heard the commotion of many people going by so he asked someone, "What's going on?" Someone answered, "Jesus of Nazareth is passing by."

Suddenly Bartimaeus began to call out, "Jesus, Son of David, have mercy on me!" Some people told him to be quiet, but he just shouted louder, "Jesus, Son of David, have mercy on me!"

Jesus stopped and said, "Tell him to come over here."
Some of the people watching said, "Bartimaeus, get up!
He's calling you!" Bartimaeus jumped to his feet and
came to Jesus.

248

"What do you want Me to do for you?" Jesus asked. Bartimaeus said, "Master, I want to see." "Go," said Jesus. "Your faith has made you well."

Immediately Bartimaeus could see and he followed
Jesus down the road, praising God.

Another time when Jesus was passing through Jericho, there was a rich tax collector who wanted to see Him. The man, named Zacchaeus, was very short and couldn't see over the crowds.

So, Zacchaeus ran ahead of the crowd that was waiting for Jesus and climbed up in a sycamore tree so he could get a good look at Him.

252

As Jesus was passing by that tree, He looked up and said, "Zacchaeus, come on down. I want to stay at your house today." So Zacchaeus hurried down, and excitedly took Jesus to his home.

Some of the people who saw this began to grumble.
"Jesus is staying with a tax collector, a sinner!"

254

But inside the house, Zacchaeus was saying, "Lord, I will give half of all I own to the poor. And, if I have cheated anyone I will pay him back four times more!"

Jesus announced, "Salvation has come to this house today. Here was a lost son of Abraham and the Messiah has come to find and save lost souls like him."